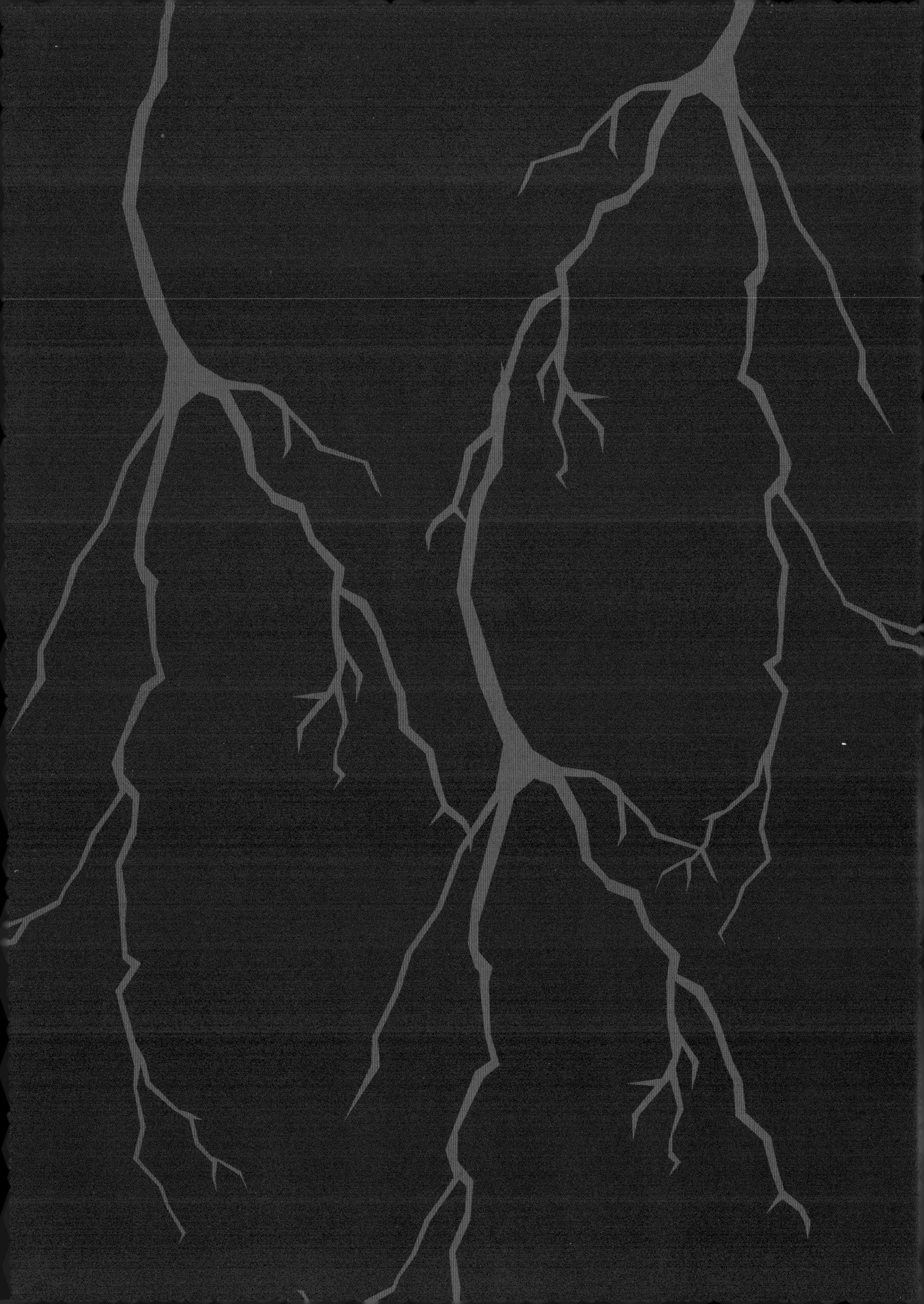

MARVEL

THOR

BEGINNINGS

Based on the Marvel comic book series The Avengers
Adapted from The Mighty Thor: Beginnings *written by* Alexandra West
Illustrated by Simone Boufantino, Roberto Di Salvo
and Tomasso Moscardini

Published by Scholastic Australia in 2017.

Scholastic Australia Pty Limited
PO Box 579 Gosford NSW 2250
ABN 11 000 614 57
www.scholastic.com.au

Part of the Scholastic Group
Sydney • Auckland • New York • Toronto
London • Mexico City • New Delhi
Hong Kong • Buenos Aires • Puerto Rico

ISBN 978-1-74299-247-1

Printed in China by RR Donnelley.

Scholastic Australia's policy, in association with RR Donnelley, is to use papers that are renewable and made efficiently from wood grown in responsibly managed forests, so as to minimise its environmental footprint.

10 9 8 7 6 5 4 3 2 18 19 20 21 / 1

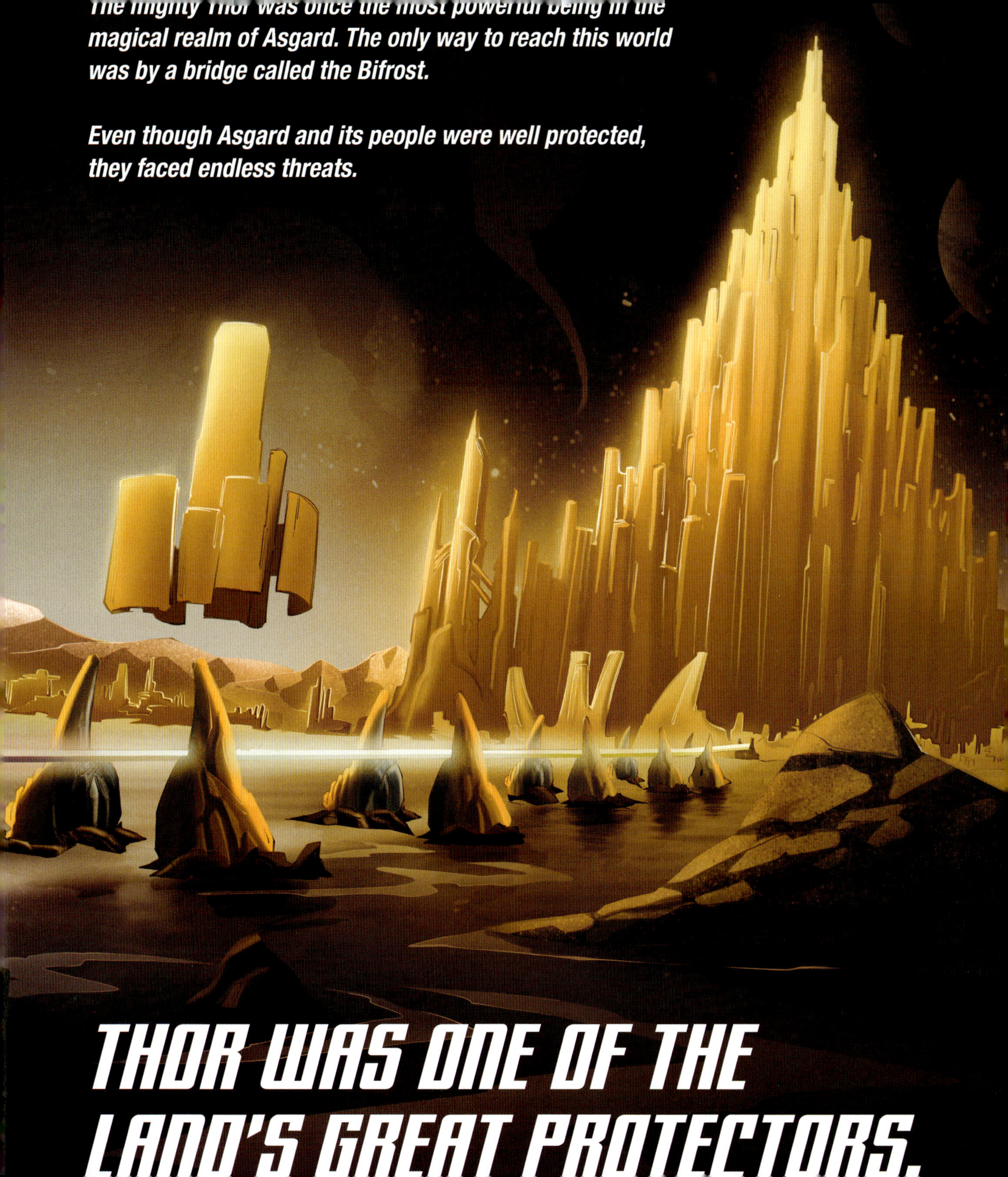
The mighty Thor was once the most powerful being in the magical realm of Asgard. The only way to reach this world was by a bridge called the Bifrost.
Even though Asgard and its people were well protected, they faced endless threats.
THOR WAS ONE OF THE LAND'S GREAT PROTECTORS.

Thor was born the son of Odin, Lord of the Asgard Gods—which meant he was a prince. He and his brother Loki, the adopted son of Odin, lived in a grand palace.

As children, Thor and Loki each wanted to prove their worth to their father. But Loki always felt that Thor was the favoured son.

Loki grew jealous of his brother. He
knew that the throne to Asgard would
one day be given to Thor. It was Thor's
right by birth.

It was important for Odin to work out when Thor would be ready to rule over Asgard. So he had a special hammer forged from a mystical metal taken from the heart of a dying star.

THE HAMMER WAS NAMED MJOLNIR!

Mjolnir held great power. But not everybody could lift the hammer . . . only a person who was proved to be worthy could pick it up.
Thor could perform amazing acts of bravery and nobility. He displayed great strength . . . but he was unable to lift the hammer.

After every great achievement, Thor would try once more to pick up Mjolnir—but he failed, time and time again. He was starting to think that he'd never be able to lift the hammer.
One day, Thor grasped Mjolnir, just as he'd done so many times before . . . and raised it high up into the air! Finally Thor had proved himself worthy of his weapon, and he used it well.
WHOOSH!

WHAM!

Odin could see that Thor had become a great warrior and had earned the respect of everyone on Asgard. But Odin wasn't happy. Thor had started to let all the attention and power go to his head.
Odin decided it was time to teach his son an important lesson . . . he cursed Thor and sent him to live on Earth as a mere mortal.

Odin made his son believe that he was a medical student with an injured leg named Don Blake. As Don, Thor helped people. He learned to study hard and passed his medical degree. Thor also allowed others to help him with his leg injury. In doing so, he learned to truly love humanity.

One day, while on holiday in Norway, Don discovered a strange walking stick inside a cave. When he struck the stick against the ground it magically transformed . . . it was Mjolnir in disguise!

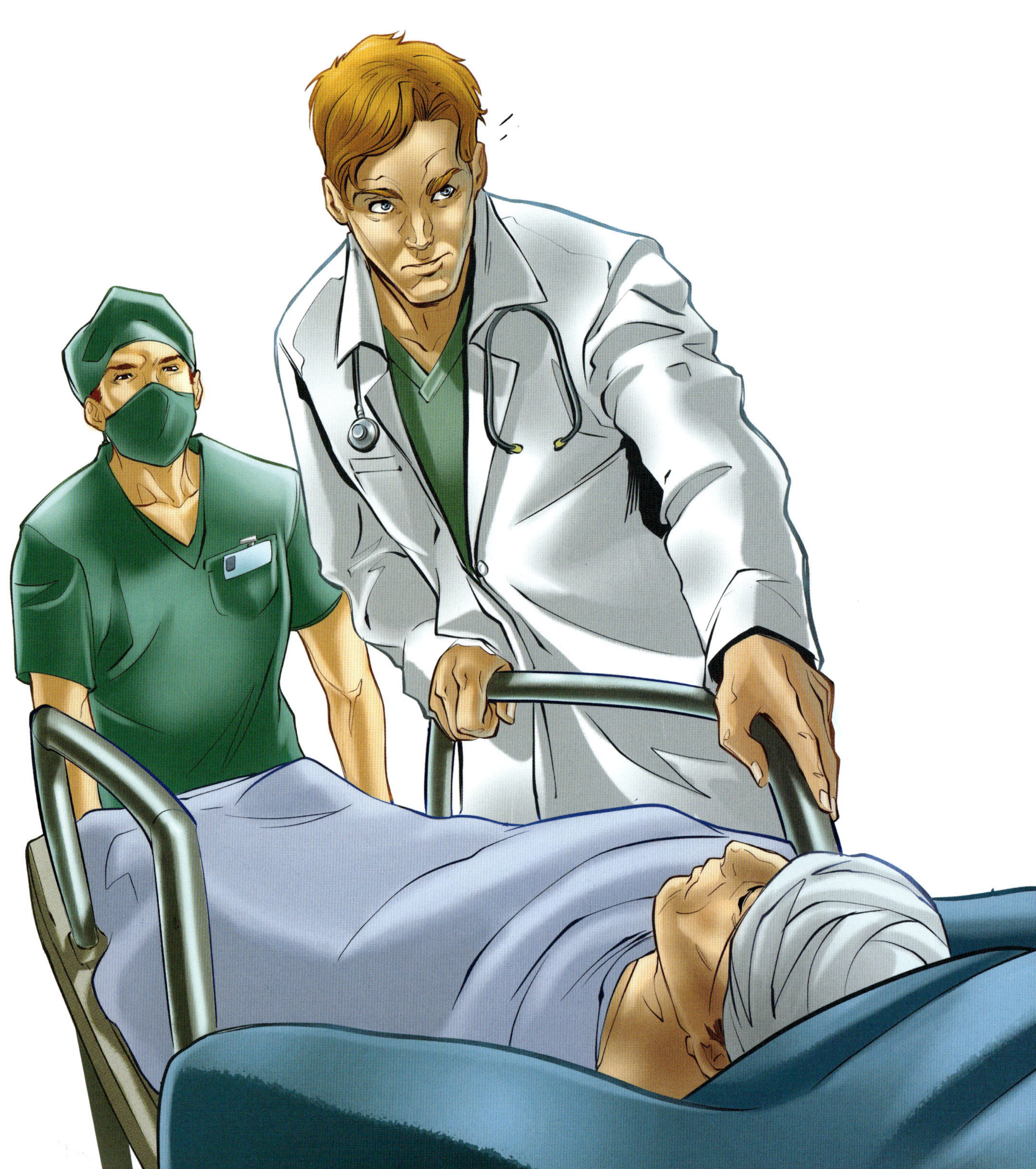

THE CURSE WAS LIFTED!

Odin was pleased. Thor had become human in spirit and had learned humility. He stayed on Earth and carried on helping people by . . .

FIGHTING CRIME AND EVIL.

THOR WAS
MIGHTY AGAIN!

While Thor fought Super Villains all over the world, his efforts attracted the attention of his jealous brother.

Loki had become Asgard's master of mischief. He was now a powerful trickster who could conjure up illusions. Loki came up with a plan that would help him defeat his older brother and prove that he was the best after all.

Loki tricked the Incredible Hulk into a fit of rage—which he knew would draw Hulk and Thor into battle. Once Thor found out that the Hulk had been manipulated by Loki, he realised he needed extra help to deal with his brother.

With the assistance of Iron Man, Hulk, Ant-Man and the Wasp, the Super Heroes combined their powers and defeated Loki. They forced him to confess his crimes.

Thor wanted to continue his work, protecting the people of Earth and
Asgard from all forms of evil—including powerful, monstrous beasts!

But Thor had learned that he
didn't have to save the world
all by himself.

It's much better to work with others to combine
STRENGTH AND
SUPER POWERS!

Thor became part of the mightiest team of Super Heroes the universe had ever witnessed. They called themselves . . .
THE AVENGERS!
THE END

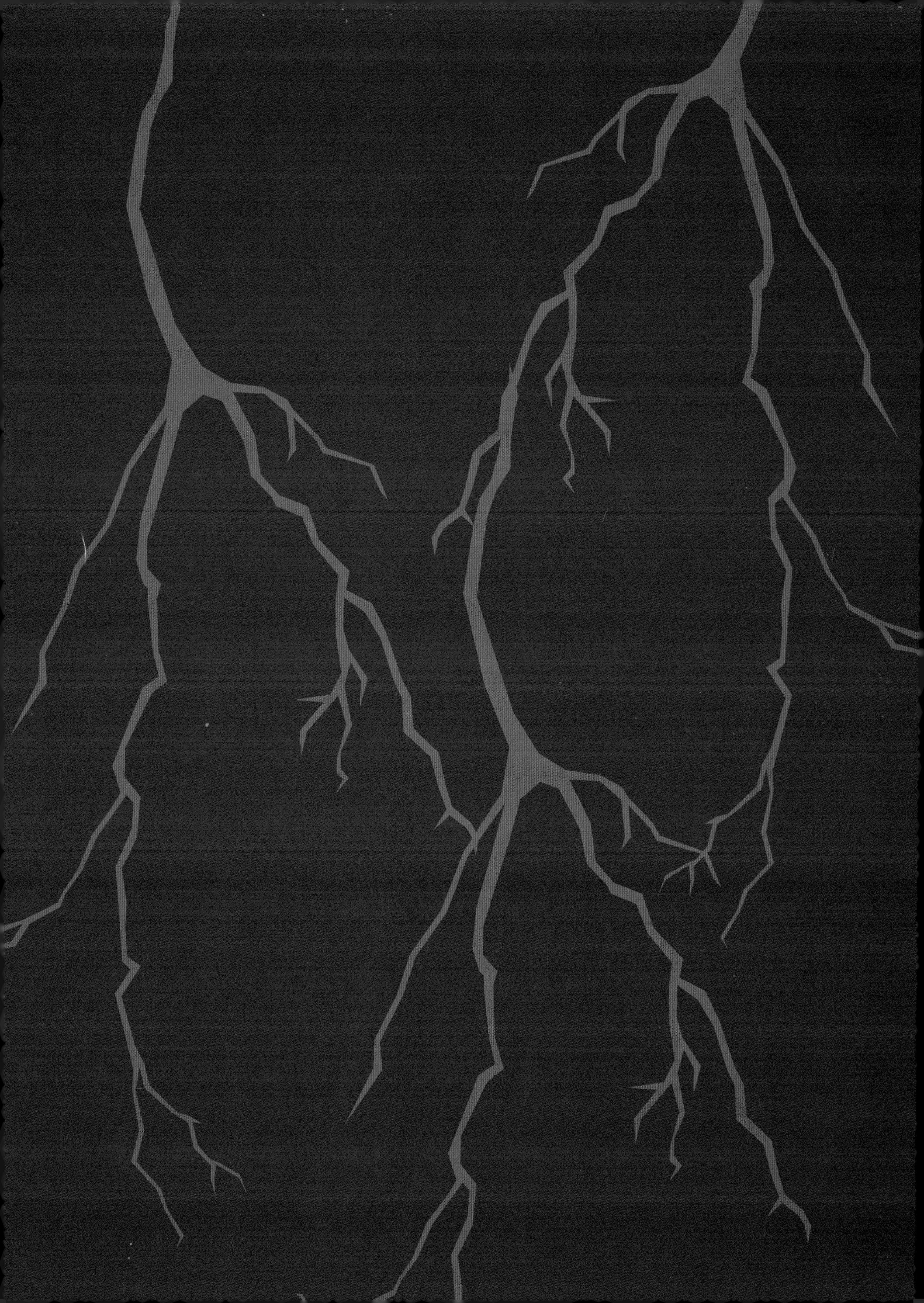